D1410832

I Tricked You!

By Phyllis Forbes Kerr

SIMON AND SCHUSTER BOOKS FOR YOUNG READERS

Published by Simon & Schuster Inc.

New York • London • Toronto • Sydney • Tokyo • Singapore

SIMON AND SCHUSTER BOOKS FOR YOUNG READERS
Simon & Schuster Building
Rockefeller Center
1230 Avenue of the Americas
New York, New York 10020

Manufactured in the United States of America

10 9 8 7 6 5 4 3 2 1

Library of Congress Cataloging-in-Publication Data
Kerr, Phyllis Forbes. I tricked you! Summary: Although Morris likes to play tricks and act silly, the other mice at school don't appreciate his antics. [1. Behavior—Fiction. 2. Mice—Fiction.] I. Title. PZ7.K46845Mo 1990 [E]—dc20
89-21795

ISBN 0-671-69408-1

To my cousin
Michael

Morris was a gray mouse with black ears.
When he was old enough his mother took
him to school.

From the first day of school he liked to play tricks.

Every morning the other mice put their coats and
lunch boxes neatly in their cubby holes, but not Morris.
He threw everything on the floor.

He raced into the classroom,

said, "Boo!" to Ms. Mousebaum,

and jumped up and down
like a wild kangaroo.

TURTLES CACTUS FISH

PUZZLES BOOKS SCISSORS CRAYONS PENCILS

Morris liked to play with building blocks,
but when it was time to put them away, he crawled
onto the shelf where the blocks belonged and
pretended to fall asleep.

BLOCKS

At snack time Morris sat beside Martha.
When she wasn't looking, he hid her cheese.
"My cheese!" moaned Martha.
"Ha, ha! I tricked you," laughed Morris,
and he gave it back.

At recess time Morris had trouble finding his jacket, so he was always last in line. He loved the playground. There he could squeak loudly, jump hard, and run fast. No one minded....

....except when he crashed into somebody.
"Ow! Watch out, Morris!" the mice squealed.

At art time Ms. Mousebaum gave everyone
scissors and paper. Morris snipped his paper
into tiny pieces and threw them up in the air.
Wheee! He thought it was great fun.
But nobody else did.

At music time Morris drowned out everybody
else. When it was his turn to play the tambourine,
he beat it so hard that the other mice said their
ears hurt.

When Morris painted, drips went everywhere.
He put the brushes in the wrong cans.
Once he even painted the easel.

At the end of the day Ms. Mousebaum read a story. But Morris was so busy with his next trick he couldn't listen. No one noticed until the story was over. Then Morris really got into trouble.

One day at playtime no
one would play with Morris.
"We're sick and tired of your
tricks, Morris," said Mackie,
as the others looked on.

"Who cares!" declared Morris
loudly. And he marched off to
play by himself.

When Morris sat down for his snack, everyone moved to another table. "We've had enough of your silly tricks," hissed Martha.

"Who cares!" said Morris proudly.

At story time everyone sat far away from him. "No one wants you or your dumb tricks," sneered Annie.

"Who cares!" snapped Morris, and he sat alone.

When Morris got on the bus, everyone moved
away.

"Who cares!" he muttered. He sat in a big seat
and looked out the window. But he couldn't see,
because his eyes were filling with tears.

When Morris got off the bus, Martha passed by
and whispered in his ear, "I think you do care."
Morris stomped his feet all the way home,
muttering, "Who cares? Not me! Who cares?
Not me!" But he knew Martha was right.
He really did care.

The next morning Morris didn't want to go
to school. No one liked his tricks and he had no
friends. He sat in bed and thought and thought.

Suddenly Morris jumped out of bed. He put
on clothes he had never worn to school before.
He found a yellow hat to cover his black ears and
wore a pair of dark glasses.

Then he examined his disguise in the mirror.
"This is going to be the best trick ever!" he said.

He arrived at school
early and put his vest
and lunch box in an
empty cubby hole.

He walked quietly
into the classroom.

"Hi! I'm Michael. I'm new," he told Ms. Mousebaum.

"Welcome, Michael," smiled the teacher. "Would you like to take off your hat and glasses?"

"No, I like them on," said Morris quickly. Ms. Mousebaum gave him a strange look.

When it was time to pick up the blocks,
Morris put them neatly on the shelf where
he usually pretended to sleep.

At snack time Morris sat quietly beside Martha.
Instead of grabbing her cheese, he ate his food
and left his place nice and neat.

When it was time for recess, Morris led the way.
He played happily with the other mice, and he was
careful not to crash into anyone.

At music time Morris sang
in a clear, sweet voice.

He kept the rhythm by playing the triangle,
evenly tapping the beat. The teacher smiled
at Morris.

At story time Morris sat between two mice
and listened to the story, which was very scary.

After the story, when it was almost time to go home,
Morris stood up. "I have a surprise for everyone."
he said. "Do you know who's missing today?"
All the mice called out, "Morris, Morris isn't here!"
"Hurray!" yelled Martha.

"Well, you're wrong; I tricked you all!"
Morris took off his dark glasses and snatched
off his yellow hat. Up popped his black ears.
Everyone gasped with surprise.

Ms. Mousebaum smiled. "You were so good, Morris," she said.

"We liked playing with you today!" said some of the mice.

"And I liked having my snack with you!" chimed in Martha.

Morris thought for a minute. It had been a nice day. He had enjoyed listening to the story. He had had fun singing and playing at recess. But most of all he had had fun playing with the other mice. They really seemed to like him.

"I had lots of fun too," beamed Morris.
"It sure was a good trick!"
He was already looking forward to the next day.

J
E
KER   31735

Ke   llis Forbes

I

JE
KER   2nd card   31735

Kerr, Phyllis Forbes
I Tricked You